Dear Parent:
Your child's love of reading starts here!

Every child learns to read in a different way and at his or her own speed. Some go back and forth between reading levels and read favorite books again and again. Others read through each level in order. You can help your young reader improve and become more confident by encouraging his or her own interests and abilities. From books your child reads with you to the first books he or she reads alone, there are I Can Read Books for every stage of reading:

SHARED READING
Basic language, word repetition, and whimsical illustrations, ideal for sharing with your emergent reader

BEGINNING READING
Short sentences, familiar words, and simple concepts for children eager to read on their own

READING WITH HELP
Engaging stories, longer sentences, and language play for developing readers

READING ALONE
Complex plots, challenging vocabulary, and high-interest topics for the independent reader

ADVANCED READING
Short paragraphs, chapters, and exciting themes for the perfect bridge to chapter books

I Can Read Books have introduced children to the joy of reading since 1957. Featuring award-winning authors and illustrators and a fabulous cast of beloved characters, I Can Read Books set the standard for beginning readers.

A lifetime of discovery begins with the magical words **"I Can Read!"**

Visit www.icanread.com for information
on enriching your child's reading experience.

For Theo and Scarlet—keep on singing!
—R.S.

I Can Read Book® is a trademark of HarperCollins Publishers.

Splat the Cat: Splat the Cat Sings Flat
Copyright © 2011 by Rob Scotton

www.icanread.com

Library of Congress Cataloging-in-Publication Data is available.
ISBN 978-0-06-197854-8 (trade bdg.) — ISBN 978-0-06-197853-1 (pbk.)

11 12 13 LP/WOR 10 9 8 7 6 5 4 3 2

❖

First Edition

I Can Read!

BEGINNING 1 READING

Splat the Cat
Sings Flat

Based on the bestselling books
by Rob Scotton

Cover art by Rob Scotton

Text by Chris Strathearn

Interior illustrations by Robert Eberz

HARPER
An Imprint of HarperCollinsPublishers

Splat the cat goes to Cat School.

Splat likes to take Seymour.

Seymour is Splat's pet mouse.

Seymour rides in Splat's hat.

One morning,

Splat's teacher had big news.

She asked all the cats

to sit on the big red mat.

Seymour sat in Splat's hat.

6

"All of you will sing
on Parents' Night,"
Mrs. Wimpydimple said.
"If your singing is loud,
your parents will be proud."

"Will lots of parents be there?"
asked Splat.

"Yes. All the parents,"
said Mrs. Wimpydimple.

"Gulp!" said Splat.

MUSIC

Splat's tail wiggled wildly.

Splat was worried.

Splat was shy.

"I can't sing," said Splat.

"Can you meow?" asked his teacher.

"I forget how to meow," said Splat.

"Can you hum?" asked his teacher.

"I even forget how to hum," said Splat.

"That's okay, Splat,"
said Mrs. Wimpydimple.
"I will help you sing.
We will all help you sing."

Mrs. Wimpydimple sang first.

"La-la-la!" she sang.

The cats on the mat began to sing.

All except Splat.

"Now you try, Splat,"
said Mrs. Wimpydimple.
Splat opened his mouth.
Nothing came out.

"You can do it, Splat,"
said his teacher.
Splat tried hard,
but all that came out
was a little squeak.

Splat looked at Seymour.

Seymour was brave.

He was a mouse

in a room full of cats.

Splat could be brave, too.

Splat opened his mouth again.

"La!" sang Splat.

The note was loud.

It was long.

And it was very, very flat!

The cats on the mat went wild.

Splat was not trying to be funny,

but he was funny anyway.

"Sing just like that!"
said Mrs. Wimpydimple.
"You will be the star
with a mouse in his hat!"
"Maybe," said Splat.

Splat went home after school.

"What if I forget my part?"

Splat asked Mom and Dad.

"You won't forget,"

they said to Splat.

"Maybe I will forget,"

said Splat.

Splat put Seymour on his head.

Splat's tail wiggled

and Seymour jiggled.

Splat sang "la!"

The note still came out flat.

"Maybe I won't forget,"
said Splat.

Soon it was Parents' Night.

All the parents came

to Splat's classroom.

The class stood on the big red mat.

"Let's begin!" said Mrs. Wimpydimple.

The class started to sing.

"La-la-la!" sang the cats.

But Splat stayed quiet.

He waited for his turn.

Mrs. Wimpydimple gave Splat a nod.

Splat was ready.

Seymour jumped onto Splat's head.

Seymour was ready, too.

Splat's tail wiggled wildly.

Splat opened his mouth very wide.

"La!" sang Splat,

and the note was flat.

It was very flat and very loud.

He opened his mouth even wider.

"LA!" sang Splat.

Then he opened his mouth

as wide as it could go.

"LAAA!" sang Splat,

and he fell off the mat.

SPLAT!

The class giggled.

The parents laughed.

And Splat laughed

the loudest of all.

"You were the star!"

said Splat's mom.

"We are very proud of you,"

said Splat's dad.

"Splat was the cat's meow!"
said Mrs. Wimpydimple.

Splat was happy.

"Guess what," said Splat.

"I didn't forget to sing flat!
I forgot to be shy."

Mom and Dad hugged Splat.

"We love our cat who sings flat."